Nora Perry

New Songs and Ballads

Nora Perry

New Songs and Ballads

ISBN/EAN: 9783744784122

Printed in Europe, USA, Canada, Australia, Japan

Cover: Foto ©Andreas Hilbeck / pixelio.de

More available books at **www.hansebooks.com**

BY

NORA PERRY
AUTHOR OF "AFTER THE BALL." "FOR A WOMAN," ETC.

BOSTON
TICKNOR AND COMPANY
1887

CONTENTS.

NEW SONGS AND BALLADS.

THE OLD YEAR TO THE NEW.

With hands full of gifts and cheeks like a rose,

There you wait

At my gate

While my winter wind blows;

And you laugh, as you stand there, a laugh full

of scorn,

At the sight

Of the plight

Of the graybeard forlorn,

And the stories he tells of the months that have

sped:

"What, I — I,"

You cry,

"When my twelve months have fled,

"To bend and to totter, to sigh and to shake,

And like you

There to rue

The vows that I break?

"Not I, oh, not I," you scornfully say;

"I shall stand

Where you stand,

As blithe as to-day,

" When one after one my twelve months have
    sped ;

    Not a fear,

    Not a tear,

Shall I murmur or shed."

So, my youngster, you laugh, as you stand
    there untried,

    As you wait

    At my gate

In your ignorant pride.

So I boasted and laughed when I stood in your
    place ;

    But to-day,

    Ah ! to-day,

At the end of my race,

I count up the gifts that I sold for a song.

In that time

Of my prime,

When lusty and strong,

My plans were so easy, my promises rife,

And pleasure

The measure

And limit of life.

But my easy-laid plans not so easily sped,

And alas!

And alas!

Ere the twelve months had fled,

I found what my fine boasted wisdom was
  worth,
        And that haste
        Had made waste
    On my kingdom of earth.

But what use for me here to counsel and pray,
        When you heed
        Not indeed
    A word that I say,

When impatient you wait for my gate to unclose,
        With that air
        Debonair,
    And that cheek like a rose!

Well, well, enter in — the gates are flung wide:

There or here,

God is near,

Whatsoever betide.

PROMISE AND FULFILMENT.

I.

WHEN the February sun

Shines in long slant rays, and the dun

Gray skies turn red and gold,

And the winter's cold

Is touched here and there

With the subtle air

That seems to come

From the far-off home

Of the orange and palm,

With their breath of balm,

And the bluebird's throat

Swells with a note

Of rejoicing gay,

Then we turn and say,

   "Why, Spring is near!"

II.

When the first fine grass comes up

In pale green blades, and the cup

Of the crocus pushes its head

Out of its chilly bed,

And purple and gold

Begins to unfold

In the morning sun,

While rivulets run

Where the frost had set

Its icy seal, and the sills are wet

With the drip, drip, drip,

From the wooden lip

Of the burdened eaves

Where the pigeon grieves,

And coos and woos,

And softly sues,

Early and late,

Its willing mate,

Then with rejoicing gay

We turn and say,

   "Why, Spring is here!"

III.

When all the brown earth lies

Beneath the blue bright skies,

Clothed with a mantle of green,

A shining, varying sheen,

And the scent and sight of the rose,

And the purple lilac-blows,

Here, there, and everywhere,

Meet one and greet one till

One's senses tingle and thrill

With the heaven and earth born sweetness,

The sign of the earth's completeness,

Then lifting our voices we say,

"Oh, stay, thou wonderful day!

Thou promise of Paradise,

That to heart and soul doth suffice.

Stay, stay! nor hasten to fly

When the moon of thy month goes by,

For the crown of the seasons is here, —

June, June, the queen of the year!"

THE SECRETS OF THE SPRING.

Come out and hear the robins sing,
And hear the bluebirds' tale of spring,
And see the swallows on the wing.

Come out and listen, listen low,
And hear the grasses as they grow,
And list the little winds that blow,

And learn to read their secret well, —
The secret that they softly tell
To bird and bee in drowsy dell,

Of bloomy banks that are to be,

Of fragrant field and leafy tree,

And all the summer mystery

Of bud and blossom, flower and fruit,

That quickens now in sap and root,

And now in tender springing shoot.

Come out, come out, the days are long,

But Nature sings her secret song

In secret ways,—the days are long;

But swift as sweet from day to day,

From hour to hour, the tuneful lay

Runs headlong on a changeful way.

Come out, then, in the early glow

Of early springtime's bud and blow, —

Come out and hear the grasses grow,

And all the secrets of the spring

That melt and murmur, speak and sing,

To ears attuned to listening.

MARCH WINDS.

WHEN rough and wild the March winds blow,
Beneath the ice we look, and lo!
We see the brooks begin to flow.

When wilder yet the wild winds sing,
We hark and hear the bluebird ring
His silver trumpet of the spring.

No bitter winds can him dismay;
Though icy currents check the way,
He scents to-morrow in to-day.

He knows that what hath been shall be;

He doth not wait as we to see

The bloom and bud upon the tree,

To measure out his joyful song;

Though bud and bloom be hidden long,

His faith is sure, his hope is strong.

APRIL THE HANDMAIDEN.

LET March have his say

For a day —

Crack his cheeks as he blows

Wind and snows

Over valley and hill

At his will:

Let March have his say;

But one day,

'Mid his winds and his snows,

Ere he knows,

He will hear my feet
As they beat
On the dust of his hills,
By his rills;
He will see my face
In its place,
Through the mist and the dew
Shining through.
" What, you," he will shout,
" Think to rout
The lion in his path
And his wrath?
You, the handmaid of May,
Think to stay
My will and my power
In this hour? "

Then on mountain and hill,

    Sharp and shrill,

I shall hear the north

    Wind pouring forth

In its might, to o'erthrow

    And lay low

Me, the handmaid of May,

    On my way.

But swift I shall leap,

    As from sleep,

And blow from my mouth

    The sweet south,

And drench the dry plain

    With my rain;

And to conquer at length

    All the strength

Of my foolish fierce foe

I 'll let go

All the warmth of my soul,

As I roll

Back the veil I had spun

From the sun.

Then I look for my foe,

And lo!

Nor on mountain or plain

Will he reign;

But somewhither, somewhere,

On the air,

I shall hear his " Godspeed and good-day,

O handmaid of May!"

THE SONG OF MAY.

MARCH and April, go your way!
You have had your fitful day;
Wind and shower, and snow and sleet,
Make wet walking for my feet, —

For I come unsandalled down
From the hillsides bare and brown;
But wherever I do tread,
There I leave a little thread

Of bright emerald, softly set .
Like a jewel in the wet;

And I make the peach-buds turn

Pink and white, until they burn

Rosy red within their cells;

Then I set the bloomy bells

Of the flowery alder ringing,

And the apple-blossoms swinging

In a shower of rosy snow,

As I come and as I go

On my gay and jocund way, —

I, the merry Princess May.

ROSES.

BLOW, roses, blow
Your pink and snow,
Your gold and red,
Ere June hath fled.

Your time is brief
For bud and leaf;
But in your hour
Of perfect flower,

Who doth not wait
Upon your state;

Who doth not own
That you alone

Hold Beauty's dower
From flower to flower,
And reign alone
On Beauty's throne?

What though your stay
Be but a day?
Your bloom and breath
Survive your death,

Haunt all the year,
So sweet, so dear
You made the day
Of your brief stay.

So, seeming dead,

Some brief lives shed

After their close

Sweets like the rose.

3

THE DAY LILY.

Just for a day, for a day
  I break into bloom, —
Just for a day, for a day
  I shed my perfume.

Just for a day, for a day —
  "Alack and alas,
How fleeting and brief thy stay!"
  They cry as I pass.

But, fleeting and brief, I give
  The wealth of my soul,

Just for the day that I live,

    Without stint or control.

What more can a life bestow,

    Though it last but a day,

Than all of its warmth and glow

    Ere it passes away?

SUMMER'S DECAY.

WHEN my first roses shed
Their petals, and lay dead,
I knew my foe Decay
Had struck at my sweet day
Of summer breath and bloom.
I heard my knell of doom
Sung by the sighing trees
With every wandering breeze.

And then and there I seemed
To see as one who dreamed

A long procession pass
Across the springing grass, —
Sweet ghosts of the dead flowers
That bloomed in last year's hours.
And stately at the head,
All clad in white and red,

Shedding their dewy scent,
My fair June darlings went;
And following after, stept
My lilies, who had kept
Their garments white as snow,
While their warm hearts did glow
With all the golden fire
That summer suns inspire.

All blooms and blossoms fair

Followed and followed there,

Until I did behold,

White as the stars, and cold,

My pale chrysanthemums pass;

And then I knew, alas!

The end had come; and knew,

While still the warm winds blew,

My darlings of to-day

Like this were on their way

To join the ghostly throng;

Like this would move along,

Pale visions, dead and dear,

To haunt another year.

Shuddering, I moaned and wept,

And in that moment crept

Shadows of storm and night

Across my summer light.

"What is my summer pride?"

Moaning, I wept and cried;

"Why do I hold my way,

If only to decay?"

Then suddenly I heard

Amid my boughs a bird

Lifting a heavenly voice.

"Rejoice, and yet rejoice,"

He sang, and sang again:

" Out of this earth-bound pain,

Out of this dread decay,

I lift my heavenly lay."

Higher and higher still,

Sweet with a sweeter thrill,

Lifted that heavenly song.

Borne on its wings along,

I saw the bloom and birth

Of the new heaven and earth;

And all my flowery host,

Each sweet departing ghost,

Seemed in my ears to sing,

" No fair and beauteous thing,

Nothing of precious cost,

Nothing we love, is lost."

TO–MORROW.

To-morrow, and to-morrow,
   Oh, fair and far away
What treasures lie, when hope is high
   Along your shining way.

What promises fulfilled,
   What better deeds to do
Than ever yet, are softly set
   Beneath your skies of blue.

To-morrow, and to-morrow,
   Oh, sweet and far away,

Still evermore lead on before

Along your shining way.

Still evermore lift up our eyes

Above what we have won,

To higher needs, and finer deeds

That we have left undone.

YOUTH AND AGE.

"So slow, so slow," one cried,
  "The hours creep by!"
"So swift, so swift," one sighed,
  "The short years fly!"

"So sweet, so sweet," one sang,
  "These days of bloom!"
"So brief, so brief!" out rang
  A voice of doom.

One lifted, as she sung,
  A summer face,

Gold-crowned and fair and young,

With summer's grace.

One turned a weary head,

With backward gaze,

Toward the sunset red

Of dying days.

NEXT YEAR.

"NEXT year, next year!" we say,
   When come to nought
Our plans and projects gay,
   Our bright dreams, fraught

With brighter hopes, that shine
   On that far rim
Of life's horizon line,
   Where dreams lie dim

And touched with morning dew, —
   "Next year, next year!"

And while we plan anew,
　The days grow sere,

The year has fled, and lo!
　We 've left behind
The glory and the glow
　We hoped to find,

And missed again the clew
　We meant to heed, —
The cherished plan to do
　Some cherished deed.

" Next year, next year!"
　Oh, why not now,
Delaying soul, *this* year
　Keep word and vow?

Oh, why not now and here,

   Why not to-day,

Before another year

   Shall run away,

Keep word and faith or ere

   An hour's delay;

Make good the promise fair,

   To-day, to-day?

FROM DARKNESS TO LIGHT.

WHERE is the promise of the day
I thought was mine but yesterday?
       Turned cold and gray,
       Fled quite away,
No remnant can I find, no blessed ray

To cheer me with its faint fair light
Through the dark gathering night,
       That like a blight
       Seems from my sight
To shut out hope, and leave in dull despite

Hope's threatening demon, dread despair.

But, as I make my moan, somewhere

Through the thick air

I hear — ah! where? —

A tender voice that like a bell doth bear

Comfort and hope unto my soul, —

Comfort and hope and brave control.

"Though clouds do roll,

O fainting soul,"

It cries, "see, close at hand shines Heaven

thy goal."

EXPERIENCE.

SAD is her voice, but sweet;

Low doth she speak to greet

Those that do come to meet

      And walk her ways.

Low doth she speak, with stress

That ofttimes pitiless

Doth seem to new distress.

      But when the days

Pass on to make the years,

And, one by one, youth's fears

And penalty of tears

      Begin to cease,

Then doth she turn and sing,

" Courage! for lo! the King

Cometh at last to bring

　　　Thy glad release!"

HIS WILL FOR OURS.

IF only I might go,
　And you could stay,
Who love the world and know
　Your time to say
The last good-by has come, —
　If only I
Could find the heavenly home,
　Could drop and die
For you, and you could meet
　From day to day
This life that is so sweet
　To you, so gay

With earthly joys and gains,

    While mine is filled

With losses and with pains,

    That leave me chilled

And changed unto the core!

    But while I stay,

You go — thus evermore

    His will, His way,

Not ours. But ours to wait,

    Patient and still,

To learn that love, not hate,

    Follows His will.

A PRAYER.

ANOINT my eyes that I may see
Through all this sad obscurity,
This worldly mist that dims my sight,
These crowding clouds that hide the light.

Full vision, as perhaps have they
Who walk beyond the boundary way,
I do not seek, I do not ask,
But only this, — that through the mask

Which centuries of soil and sin

Have fashioned for us, I may win

A clearer sight to show me where

Truth walks with faith divine and fair.

BEHIND THE MASK.

"SHE speaks and smiles the old gay way,
She is the same as yesterday,"
   You turn and say;

The same as yesterday, before
The dark-winged angel at her door
   Entered and bore

The treasure of her life away:
"The same, the same as yesterday."
   And as you say

These questioning words with questioning tone,
Apart from you and quite alone
    She makes her moan;

Even as she stands before you there
With all the old accustomed air, —
    The smiles that wear

The mirthful mask of yesterday, —
She stands alone and far away
    From yesterday.

She stands alone and quite apart,
With mirth and song her aching heart
    Has lot nor part.

The while you criticise her air
Of gay response, pierced with despair
     She does not dare

To speak aloud her bitterness,
To tell you of her loneliness
     And sore distress.

She does not dare to trust her woe
To break its bonds, her tears to flow
     In outward show,

Lest, like a giant in her life
This woe should rise. to stronger life
     And fiercer strife.

So, wearing on her face the guise

Of olden smiles, with tearless eyes

   She dumbly tries

To lift her burden to the light,

To live by faith and not by sight,

   And from the night

Of new despair and wasting grief

At last, at last to find relief

   Beyond belief.

THE HIDDEN WAY.

OH, what was the way you took that day,
   That day that you went from me?
You called me twice, and you called me thrice,
   I heard, but I could not see.

I dared not look, for I could not brook
   To see my darling's face
Take on some strange and terrible change
   That should mar its tender grace.

You called me twice, and you called me thrice.
   My name was the very last

On your lips that day, as you went that way, —

   A way I had followed fast,

Oh, fast where'er my love did fare,

   If the hidden way I had known;

No fear had stayed, no doubts delayed,

   For I should have followed my own.

Yet even then, ah, even then,

   When you called upon my name,

You were out of reach of my touch or speech,

   And beyond my call or claim.

But even then, ah, even then

   You 'd have turned to me, my dear,

And left all heaven, had strength been given,

   To have shared my darkness here.

But vain, oh, vain, and worse than vain,

My agony or yours;

Death sends no ray to light that way,

Nor will, while Time endures.

THE CRY OF THE DOUBTER.

IF we could go some day,

Before Age claims us for his prey,

Drop out of all this strife

That we call life,

And without coward fears,

Or fainting flesh, or wasting tears,

Find suddenly the land

Of all our dreams, and stand

There, face to face with treasure lost,

The friends whose dread departure cost

Our souls such sore distress,

Such agonies of wretchedness, —

If we could go like this,
With consciousness of bliss
Set full before us, who would stay
To linger on the way
Through weary year by year
Till time was ripe and sere
With length of days and loss?
But set upon the cross
Of mystery and pain
We wait and wait again,
Perhaps through threescore years
Of doubting hopes and fears,
And at the end we say,
"Ah, what a little day
Of joy is life, and long, oh, long,
The day of pain." Then from the throng

We drop away, while others sigh,

Bending above our clay, and cry,

As we have cried, " Why should we wait like this

In darkness and in doubt; why miss

So much of life in wasting pain?"

O mystery of loss and gain,

Behind your veil what answer lies?

Is it some splendor of surprise

That consciousness might here defeat, —

Some joy too high for us to meet

One moment even, face to face,

While thus within earth's dull embrace,

The fetters of the flesh, we stand?

Are we upon the border-land

Of greater life thus blindly driven,

Lest if some sudden glimpse were given

Of that near heaven, we could not stay

To wait upon Time's slow delay,

But in some moment rash might break

The bond of flesh, and boldly take

Both law and life in eager hands,

Part once for all these mortal bands

To reach that glory, far, yet near,

That we had glimpsed, — that radiant sphere

That holds the payment of all pain?

O mystery of loss and gain,

Is this the meaning of it all, —

The doubt, the darkness, and the pall

That shuts us in? O Christ! O God!

If once you rolled away the sod

And lifted death to life for eyes

Of earth — if once that high surprise

You dared to give, for us once more,

Who languish on this barren shore

Of doubting times, whose blighting bale

Has girt us round, lift up the veil,

Roll back the sod, and give us grace

To look beyond this narrow space!

TOO LATE.

WHAT silences we keep year after year
With those who are most near to us and dear!
We live beside each other day by day,
And speak of myriad things, but seldom say
The full, sweet word that lies just in our reach,
Beneath the commonplace of common speech.

Then out of sight and out of reach they go, —
These close familiar friends, who loved us so;
And, sitting in the shadow they have left,
Alone with loneliness, and sore bereft,

We think with vain regret of some fond word

That once we might have said and they have
      heard.

For weak and poor the love that we expressed

Now seems beside the vast, sweet *un*expressed,

And slight the deeds we did, to those undone,

And small the service spent, to treasure won,

And undeserved the praise for word and deed

That should have overflowed the simple need.

This is the cruel cross of life, — to be

Full visioned only when the ministry

Of death has been fulfilled, and in the place

Of some dear presence is but empty space.

What recollected services can then

Give consolation for the " might have been "?

NECESSITY.

GAUNT-FACED and hungry-eyed she waits,
This sombre warder of our fates,
Forever sleepless while we sleep,
And silent while we moan and weep.

Sometimes, beguiled by smiling skies
And wooing winds, we shut our eyes,
Forgetting for a little space
That tireless, unforgetting face.

Or, stirred as stirs the sap in spring
By Nature's force, we laugh and sing,

Or run to pass that waiting shape
With flying footsteps of escape.

But where we run she leads the way,
She goes before us night and day;
No flying footsteps can escape,
By any path, that sombre shape.

Always she waits with whip and spur
To urge us on if we demur;
With bitter breath we call her " foe,"
As driven thus we rise and go.

The roads we follow wind and twist,
Our eyes grow blind with blinding mist,
Blown down to us as we ascend
The upland heights that near the end.

And at the end — " Where is our foe?

Where hideth she?" we cry; and lo!

Through breaking mist, an angel's face

Looks out upon us from her place!

ABRAHAM LINCOLN'S CHRISTMAS GIFT.

'T WAS in eighteen hundred and sixty four,

That terrible year when the shock and roar

Of the nation's battles shook the land,

And the fire leapt up into fury fanned, —

The passionate, patriotic fire,

With its throbbing pulse and its wild desire

To conquer and win, or conquer and die,

In the thick of the fight when hearts beat high

With the hero's thrill to do and to dare,

'Twixt the bullet's rush and the muttered prayer.

In the North, and the East, and the great North-
    west,
Men waited and watched with eager zest

For news of the desperate, terrible strife, —
For a nation's death or a nation's life;
While over the wires there flying sped
News of the wounded, the dying and dead.

"Defeat and defeat! ah! what was the fault
Of the grand old army's sturdy assault
At Richmond's gates?" in a querulous key
Men questioned at last impatiently,

As the hours crept by, and day by day
They watched the Potomac Army at bay.

Defeat and defeat! It was here, just here,

In the very height of the fret and fear,

Click, click! across the electric wire

Came suddenly flashing words of fire,

And a great shout broke from city and town

At the news of Sherman's marching down, —

Marching down on his way to the sea

Through the Georgia swamps to victory.

Faster and faster the great news came,

Flashing along like tongues of flame, —

McAllister ours!   And then, ah! then,

To that patientest, tenderest, noblest of men,

This message from Sherman came flying swift, —

"I send you Savannah for a Christmas gift!"

WENDELL PHILLIPS.

ALONG the streets one day with that swift tread
He walked a living king — then, " He is dead ! "
The whisper flew from lip to lip, while still
Sounding within our ears the echoing thrill
Of his magician's voice we seemed to hear
In notes of melody ring near and clear.

So near, so clear, men cried, " It cannot be !
It was but yesterday he spoke to me ;
But yesterday we saw him move along,
His head above the crowd, swift-paced and strong ;

But yesterday his plan and purpose sped, —

It cannot be to-day that he is dead!"

A moment thus, half-dazed, men met and spoke,

When first the sudden news upon them broke:

A moment more, with sad acceptance turned

To face the bitter truth that they had spurned.

Friends said, through tears, " How empty seems

      the town!"

And warring critics laid their weapons down.

He had his faults, they said, but they were faults

Of head and not of heart, — his sharp assaults,

Flung seeming heedless from his quivering

      bow,

And heedless striking either friend or foe,

Were launched with eyes that saw not foe or
    friend,
But only, shining far, some goal or end

That, compassed once, should bring God's sav-
    ing grace
To purge and purify the human race.
The measure that he meted out he took,
And blow for blow received without a look,
Without a sign of conscious hurt or hate
To stir the tranquil calmness of his state.

Born on the heights and in the purple bred,
He chose to walk the lowly ways instead,
That he might lift the wretched, and defend
The rights of those who languished for a friend.

So many years he spent in listening

To these sad cries of wrong and suffering,

It was not strange, perhaps, he thought the right

Could never live upon the easeful height,

Nor strange indeed that slow suspicion grew

Against the class whose tyrannies he knew.

But bitter and unsparing as his speech,

He meant alone the evil deed to reach.

No hate of persons winged his fiery shaft;

He had no hatred but for cruel craft

And selfish measurements, where human Might

Bore down upon the immemorial Right.

Even while he dealt his bitterest blows at power,

No bitterness that high heart could devour.

How at the last this great heart conquered all,

We know who watched above his sacred pall, —

One day a living king he faced a crowd

Of critic foes; over the dead king bowed

A throng of friends who yesterday were those

Who thought themselves, and whom the world

    thought, foes.

CONTRAST.

THE bells of Lent rang up, rang down,
Through all the babel of the town;
Rang soft, rang clear, rang loud or low,
As loud or low March winds did blow.

Through wide-flung doors the hurrying throng
Caught hint of psalm and snatch of song, —
The high-strung song of plaint and prayer,
Of cross, and passion, and despair.

One, hurrying by amid the throng,
Who caught the sweetness of the song

Above the turmoil of the street,
Turned suddenly her weary feet,

And through the wide-flung doors passed in
From out the week-day whirl and din.
" Call me away from flesh and sense —
Thy grace, O Lord, can draw me thence,"

In fervent tones the singers sang,
While solemnly the organ rang.
" From flesh and sense," — the words struck clear
Upon the stranger's listening ear.

"From flesh and sense." She looked across
The sunlit aisles, where glint and gloss
Of diamond-fire and satin shone, —
A princess' raiment, that had won

A prince's ransom in the past, —

Across the aisles, then downward cast

Her seeking glance in bitter heed

Of raiment that scarce met the need

That winter keen and merciless

Brought home to her with savage stress.

And they, — they neither toil nor spin,

These lilies fair, apparelled in

These costly robes, while others strive,

And mourn to find themselves alive

Beneath the burdens of the day,

That leave small time or wish to pray.

" Call me away from flesh and sense,"

When flesh itself seems half drawn thence.

" For you, for you, O favored ones,

These silken stalls, these organ tones,"

Her bitter thought ran, as the prayer

Floated in music on the air.

" For you, for you this house you call

The house of God; for me the thrall

" Of toil and toil, from day to day,

While life wastes sordidly away

In vainest hope and dull despair

Of some sweet time, when one from care

" May pause and rest a little space,

And meet life's bright things face to face.

But faint of heart, and very low

Of hope and comfort, I but know

" In these dark days the needs of earth.

All else seems now of little worth;

And little worth your silken prayer

Against my wall of dull despair."

CRESSID.

Has any one seen my Fair,
Has any one seen my Dear?
Could any one tell me where
And whither she went from here?

The road is winding and long,
With many a turn and twist,
And one could easy go wrong,
Or ever one thought or list.

How should one know my Fair,
And how should one know my Dear?

By the dazzle of sunlight hair
That smites like a golden spear.

By the eyes that say " Beware,"
By the smile that beckons you near, —
This is to know my Fair,
This is to know my Dear.

Rough and bitter as gall
The voice that suddenly comes
Over the windy wall
Where the fishermen have their homes : —

" Ay, ay, we know full well
The way your fair one went:

She led by the ways of Hell,
And into its torments sent

" The boldest and bravest here,
Who knew nor guilt nor guile,
Who knew not shadow of fear
Till he followed that beckoning smile.

" Now would you find your Fair,
Now would you find your Dear?
Go, turn and follow her where
And whither she went from here,

" Along by the winding path
That leads by the old sea-wall:
The wind blows wild with wrath,
And one could easily fall

" From over the rampart there,

If one should lean too near,

To look for the sunlight hair

That smites like a golden spear ! "

HENRY OF NAVARRE BEFORE PARIS.

DOWN upon the 'leaguered town
With forty thousand men he rode:
The fields were bare, the meadows brown,
    The starving cattle faintly lowed.

But conquering hero he rode down, —
As if to hawk and bells he rode, —
While fields were bare and meadows brown,
    And starving cattle faintly lowed.

And just without the 'leaguered town
They pitched their tents along the road,

Or in the fields and meadows brown

    Where starving cattle faintly lowed.

Day after day they stormed the town;

Day after day he laughing rode

Across the fields and meadows brown

    Where starving cattle faintly lowed.

One day from out the 'leaguered town

There faltered forth along the road,

And by the fields and meadows brown

    Where starving cattle faintly lowed,

A wretched throng. The 'leaguered town

Had cast aside its useless load,

And by the fields and meadows brown

    Where starving cattle faintly lowed,

They faltered up, they faltered down,

Half dazed with fear, along the road.

Then, by the fields and meadows brown

    Where starving cattle faintly lowed,

The hero who had stormed the town

Day after day, and careless rode,

Day after day by meadows brown

    Where starving cattle faintly lowed,

With swift, sharp strokes came riding down

Along the white and dusty road,

Unheeding still the meadows brown,

    The starving cattle as they lowed.

His face was set beneath a frown;

His laughing eyes, that had bestowed

No glance upon the meadows brown

  Where starving cattle faintly lowed,

Now fierce yet soft looked shining down

Upon the groups that thronged the road.

Blind to the meadows bare and brown,

  Deaf to the cattle as they lowed,

His great heart suddenly bore down

The conqueror's pride, and back he rode

Past all the fields and meadows brown

  Where starving cattle faintly lowed.

He fed the people of the town, —

These famished groups that thronged the road, —

And through the fields and meadows brown

  He called the cattle as they lowed,

And fed them all.   Then from the town

He turned away, and lightly rode

Past all the fields and meadows brown,

   With face that shone and eyes that glowed.

"Vive Dieu!" he cried, "I'll take no town

By famine's scourge: a fairer road

Must Henry of Navarre ride down

   To find his triumphs well bestowed."

MY PRINCESS.

SHE walks beyond me fair and far,

As yon fair ship beyond the bar

Stands out to sea, or, in delay,

At anchor rides day after day.

Day after day, before my eyes,

Just out of reach, the white sails rise:

Just out of reach, day after day,

Like this she keeps and holds her way,

Who holds and sways my heart, until

Within my soul some tenser thrill

Wakes into life, and I forget

A moment then the gulf that yet

Between us lies, the swelling sea

That separates my love from me.

My love! With bated breath I name

Her thus, yet even thus dare not proclaim

To her, before whom others kneel,

The throes of passion that I feel.

And yet — and yet, day after day,

She leads me on with looks that say

What speech denies, with smiles that prick

My armor through, though leaden thick.

The daughter of a regnant queen,

My princess fair, doth she demean

Her high estate, stoop from her place,

To lure a victim by her grace?

Even while this doubt assaileth me,

Amidst the courtly throng I see

A face that for an instant there

Seems touched with some divine despair, —

A look of human need and loss

That like a shadow flits across

The eyes whose smile but yesternight

Shone with a bright, alluring light.

Another moment, down the room

Her gay laugh rings. I catch the bloom

Of sudden roses on her cheek;

I meet her glance; I hear her speak

In jesting words, — the old light way.

But down the room the harpers play

Wild waltzes, with a dying fall

In every note, a plaintive call

Of passionate, entreating pain

Inwoven with each mirthful strain.

I listen, and remember there

The face touched with divine despair, —

I listen, lifting up my heart;

I look, where near and yet apart

She holds her way afar from me, —

Afar yet near; I look, and see

My love, though seas may roll between!

My own, though kingdoms stand between!

UNDER THE MISTLETOE.

She stood before the chimney-place,

A little maid of winsome grace,

And watched the great flames leap and dance,

With merriest mischief in her glance.

Along the floor, across the wall,

The fire's bright light did flash and fall,

And for the moment made the room

Of grimmest Puritanic gloom

Shine with a festal glow and gleam

In every nook, on every beam

Of solid oak; and on the snow
Across the road it seemed to throw

Its gay, inviting radiance,
Where oaken shutters gave a chance
From heart-shaped loopholes rudely cut,
Or from some crevice left unshut.

"Good Master Matthews holds perchance
A feast to-night," one said askance,
Who hastened by. "A feast of *saints;*
No wicked revelry attaints

"Our godly brother," answered back
A guest, who, following on the track
Of beaten snow, quick overheard
This flippant tone and jesting word.

Low laughed the merry jester there

Beneath his breath. "If I could share

Good Master Matthews' cheer to-night,"

He whispered soft, "I'd see a sight

"Worth half a year of pangs and pains,

Or priestly penance for the stains

Of heedless sins; but I, alack!

I am a foolish youth, too slack

"Of solemn sighs, too rife with mirth,

To be a Puritan of worth,

And Master Matthews' bidden guest

On such a night as this — 't is best,

"Perhaps; for if sweet Mistress Ann

Should *look* a laugh, as I'm a man

I should so follow suit, they'd gaze
And gaze at me with shocked amaze."

Meantime, within the mansion there
He passed so gayly by, this fair
And winsome Mistress Ann did face
Good Master Matthews in disgrace.

'Twas when the twenty candles' light
Flared suddenly upon a sight
Taboo to Puritanic eyes, —
"What, what!" good Master Matthews cries

With heat and haste, "this mummery *here*
Beneath *my* roof!" — "But, cousin dear,
'Tis Christmas Eve, you know, and so
This holly-wreath and mistletoe

"I brought from over seas — "   " What then?"

He swift returns.   " These godly men

And dames who are my guests to-night

Scorn all such tricks that would bedight

"Such sacred things with vain ado."

Here Mistress Ann returned: "I, too,

Good cousin, — am I not your guest,

With right to courtesy the best?"

Struck dumb with this reproach he stood.

Who hesitates is lost.   " Ah, good

My cousin, leave it all to me!"

Laughed Mistress Ann right merrily;

"I 'll take the blame, I 'll take the shame,

I promise you, and with my claim

Of latest guest from over seas
I'll stake my word I'll conquer these

"Grim Puritans, good cousin mine!
Now let us make the candles shine
Anew, for here they come." She ran
Like any deer, this Mistress Ann,

Just here, and, laughing, stood beneath
The mistletoe and holly-wreath.
The first who entered there was he
Who ruled the town, and held the key

Of state. His brow was grave, his coat
Was graver still, — once at his throat
And wrists clung ruffles of fine lace.
'T was in the old days, when a lofty place

He held at court, — the godless days
Of early youth's poor vain displays.
"My sooth, he is a goodly man,"
Under her breath quoth Mistress Ann.

" He knew my mother once, and me,
He held me once upon his knee
In childhood days," she smiling thought;
Then all at once she blushing caught

His questioning gaze. " I 'm little Ann,"
She sweetly said. The grave, stern man
At this relaxed his visage grim;
The Puritan precise and prim

Slipped like a mask, and, as he should,
He bent and kissed her where she stood.

The twenty candles flamed and flared,
The twenty guests in silence stared.

Then rose a murmur, shocked and low, —
They'd spied the branch of mistletoe!
As meek as any dove she stood,
This Mistress Ann, to breast the flood

Of blame that broke, when, "Let it pass,
She's but a child, — a foolish lass,"
A voice declared, to be obeyed.
Something within the voice betrayed

A latent laugh to Mistress Ann.
She looked, and in a moment's span
Read there behind his visage grim
Full pardon for her saucy whim.

"In sooth he is a goodly man,

And not so very grim," quoth Ann;

"He loved my mother once, and me;

He held me once upon his knee."

KING GEORGE'S TOWNS.

FROM end to end the house was filled

    With laughing guests.

From end to end the music thrilled,

    And jovial jests

From lip to lip ran gayly round,

    And light steps beat

The measures out, and light hearts found

    The measures sweet.

"Next week, next year," they smiling planned,

    As one assumes

All things secure, while softly fanned

The peacock plumes

The gay dames held, — next week, next year:

The fiddlers played

Their wildest tunes, the horns blew clear,

The banners swayed

In rhythmic movements where they hung;

All things were set

To melody, — to music strung,

And yet, and yet,

What minor chord was that he heard, —

The gallant host?

Beneath the banners where they stirred

What shadowy ghost

Was that he saw, defiant, grim,

Step darkly down

To mock the scene, and menace him
	With warning frown,
While still they planned, " next week, next year,"
	His careless guests?
They saw no ghost, they felt no fear,
	Why stop their jests

Who held beneath King George's crown
	The royal right
To hold and rule King George's town
	By loyal might?
" Next week, next year;" and while they spoke,
	Across the hum
Of horns and fiddles bluntly broke
	A rolling drum

That beat to arms the " rabble rout"

   They did disdain.

" Next week, next year," — the year ran out

   And out again,

And through and through King George's towns,

   From east to west,

From north to south, the drum-beat drowns

   The idle jest

On Tory lips. The rabble rout

   Rise fast and far;

They follow on with cheer and shout

   The morning star

Of victory's dawn. " Next week, next year!"

   Their cry rings down,

"We bend no more with cringing fear
　　'Neath George's crown!"

Behind her fan of peacock plumes
　　The Tory dame
Makes no more plans, no more assumes
　　To ban with shame
The "rabble rout" she once disdained;
　　While he, her host
Who under George's banners reigned,
　　Recalls the ghost
That once upon a festal night,
　　Defiant, grim,
Stepped darkly down athwart the light
　　To menace him!

THE CHRISTMAS GALE.

BLIND and bitter the storm beat down:
Through the streets of the little town
Women and men went hurrying fast,
Their troubled glance on the splintered mast

That pitched and tossed just off the shore
Where rocks were sharp and the tempest tore
In fiercer wrath the treacherous waves
That year by year had made the graves

Of luckless sailors bearing down
On homeward trips to the harbor town.

"Ah, God forbid," the women prayed,

As the splintered mast rose up and swayed

Like a human form against the sky, —

" Ah, God forbid that our boys should die

Like this, like this, almost in sight

Of our very eyes on Christmas night! "

Then such a cry was overheard:

" On Christmas night he gave his word

He 'd come to me," a young voice cried.

" On Christmas night last year, a bride,

" I waited in this very place,.

And saw his smiling, handsome face

On watch for me, as he looked down,

Across the bows, upon the town."

She ceased a moment, looking far

Towards the seething harbor-bar,

With eager eyes in wondering gaze.

"What ails the girl?   Has sudden craze

"O'ertaken her?" they whispered there,

Who caught her strange expectant stare.

"What ails the girl?" when — "Look and see,"

She cried in sudden ecstasy —

"They're off the rocks, they've passed the bar,

In spite of shattered sail and spar!

They're safe! they're safe! oh, God be praised!"

The crowd about her stare amazed.

No human eye the gathering dark

Could pierce like this, — but hark! oh, hark!

What sound was that along the tide?
"Fling out your ropes!" an old salt cried;

"The girl is right — they've passed the bar,
They're coming in!"   A loud huzza
Went out and up from forty throats;
Then into line they swung their boats,

And boat to boat, with guard and gird
Of seasoned rope, without a word
They held their place, the trusty score
Of gray old salts, till close to shore

They caught the sound, they saw the sight
They'd waited for, and hoarse delight
Rang out again in lusty notes
Along the line of waiting boats.

Then swift and sharp the orders rang,

And " Hard, pull hard," the sailors sang;

And sailors' voices answered back,

From out the driving wreck and rack.

And into port there came at last,

With battered hull and splintered mast

And ragged sails, the sloop " Annette."

Not soon will those who watched forget

The girl-wife's face as full in view

She saw her captain and his crew;

Nor soon forget the words they heard, —

" *God would not let him break his word!* "

When summer suns bring strangers down

To roam about the harbor town,

The gray old salts now tell the tale
Of what befell that Christmas gale,

And gazing dreamily afar
Toward the line of harbor-bar,
They whisper in the fading light,
"It was a miracle of sight,

"For never any eye before
Could see like that across the shore;
And never any sail came down
Like that into our harbor town."

THE FAMINE.

ALL along the meadow-land
  The rain beat and beat,
And up aloft the orchard croft,
  And in among the wheat,

And where the corn was standing green,
  And where the oats were white,
Day after day, day after day.
  And through the dreary night

The driving flood came down and down,
  Until in sore despair

The people cried, "God stay the tide,
    And let His winds blow fair."

For blight was gathering on the wheat,
    And mildew on the corn,
The oats hung down in rotting brown,
    The rye-fields bent forlorn.

But day by day the lowering clouds
    Poured forth their floods, until
The evil spell of hunger fell,
    And famine had its will.

Then rose a cry that went to heaven
    And opened all its doors,
And hurrying forth from South, from North,
    And up from distant shores,

The agents of the Lord came swift
  To succor and to save;
With corn and wheat the ships sailed fleet
  Across the ocean wave.

Then ceased the wailing cry of woe,
  The dread note of despair,
And hand clasped hand from strand to strand,
  And curses changed to prayer.

Then knit the tie of brotherhood,
  And love sprang into birth,
Where scorn and spleen had come between
  These nations of the earth.

THANKSGIVING DAY.

PILE up, pile up the lordly logs,
　　November winds are high,
And daylight dies with swift surprise
　　Across the sunset sky.

But kindling flames upon the hearth
　　Shall set to sweetest tune
The wandering wail that haunts the gale
　　With melancholy rune.

Pile up then maple, birch, and pine,
　　And bring the ancient fare

They loved of old, — the russets gold,

    And cider clear and rare.

And heap a dish with hardier fruit,

    And crack the walnuts well,

Then round the fire draw nigh and nigher,

    And yield unto the spell, —

The spell of old Thanksgiving days,

    That from the ancient past

Pleads with us here to hold good cheer

    While life and love shall last.

And let us pledge those bold, brave hearts

    Who, in their reverent way,

With simple state did consecrate

    Their first Thanksgiving Day.

Hard was their lot through dreary months,
  And difficult their toil,
And at the best they did but wrest
  From out the virgin soil

A scanty harvest at the end;
  But thankful hearts were theirs,
And scanty fare, if each man's share,
  Was sweetened by their prayers.

High-souled and stanch of faith and zeal,
  Simple, sincere, devout,
They held their way from day to day
  Untroubled by a doubt.

No evil times could shake their trust;
  Alike they thanked their Lord,

And praised His will, through good and ill,

    With frank and sweet accord.

Full far and wide our harvests spread,

    Where theirs were scant and mean;

Full far and wide our prosperous tide

    Of plenty can be seen.

Our land is glutted for our greed,

    With waste is overspent,

But ever yet we moan and fret

    With peevish discontent.

Oh, sweet, brave souls, wherever now

    You walk beyond our sight,

Show us to-day your nobler way

    And lift us to your light.

Rouse up our sleeping, sluggish hearts,

Break up the worldly crust,

Teach us to feel your kindling zeal,

Your faith and hope and trust.

THE PURITAN EASTER.

TEMP. 1676.

I.

WHILE yet the dawn was faint and gray,

Before the breaking of the day,

Across the town she took her way.

Her step was light as any doe;

So swift she went there scarce did show

A print upon the crust of snow.

So swift she went, so light and swift

Against the gray dawn's murky rift,

Her slender figure seemed to lift—

A phantom form of ghostly height,

That struck with sudden, sore affright

And wondering awe the luckless wight

Who chanced her way. " A wraith ! " he cried

In faltering tones, then onward hied

In mighty fear, nor looked aside

To right or left. He did not hear,

As on he fled in shivering fear,

Her mocking laugh ring low and clear,

Nor hear her words: " The foolish clown !

He 's like his betters of the town,

Who fly at nought and flout a gown.

"'A wraith' indeed! if he but knew!"

She laughs again. The sky grows blue;

She turns and sees her goal in view, —

A little church all plain and prim,

Or "meeting-house" it was their whim

To call it then, — these elders grim

Who ruled the town in that old day,

With primmest Puritanic sway,

'Gainst which no voice must utter nay.

Over the threshold of the door

She entered in; across the floor

She lightly stepped; a moment more,

9

Upon the pulpit plain and bare,

Upon the oaken stand and chair,

And on the gallery rail and stair,

She hangs a wealth of leaf and spray

Such as the chill New England day

Could yield from wood and forest gray.

A cross of hemlock just beneath

A crown of thorns; and still beneath,

Like burnished gold, a shining wreath

Of immortelles. Then low she kneels;

Athwart her face a rapture steals;

With tender cry her soul appeals

To Christ the risen Lord that day.
"Whose way of thorns shall be my way,
Whose word shall be my prop and stay!"

She cries in ecstasy of joy, —
That passion born of no alloy
Of earthly hope or earthly joy.

Then swiftly as she came, she went,
Before the morning mist was spent,
Her thoughts on heavenly things intent.

II.

Aghast the elders stand, and stare
At pulpit front and oaken chair,
At gallery rail and gallery stair.

"Whose work is this?" they hoarsely cry;

"What papist hand, covert and sly,

Dares thus our godly laws defy?"

A gloomy glance goes glowering down

From man to maid, gray-haired and brown.

Gathering at last in awful frown,

It fixes on the comely face

Of one who seems to lack no grace

Of noble thought or noble race:

For who but he who came to bring

That meddling message from the king

About their laws, could do this thing?

Just at the height of all the storm,

When words raged hot, a slender form

Came swiftly forth, a stately form

That like a willow in its place

Drooped with a lovely, living grace.

Wondering, they looked upon her face.

" It was not he, but I," she said,

" Who did this thing: now turn instead

Your wrath on me, and on my head

" Bestow the burden of your blame ! "

A sudden horror crept like flame

Through all the throng, a sudden shame

That swept them from their saintly pride

Of virtuous power. What! she, the bride

Of him whose name rang far and wide

As chief of elders in the land, —

A goodly man whose righteous hand

Had snatched full many a costly brand

From out the very jaws of Hell! —

At first, as if beneath some spell,

A boding silence on them fell;

Then like a flood their horror burst.

They branded her as one accurst,

A poison viper they had nurst

Within their breasts, to turn again

And mock the simple word and plain

Of Christ the Lord by symbols vain

Of papist craft and papist guile!

She heard them through, her face the while

Gathering a strange, half-bitter smile.

" What! you," she cried, "and you, and you,

Who broke the old faith for the new,

Who made your boast that through and through

"Your new-found land men should be free

Of priestly power, or tyranny

Of Church or State; should welcome be

"To hold their faith before the day,

To serve the Lord by yea or nay

Of all the creeds,— you, you to say

" And swear me false with hasty blame

Of hasty words, that brand with shame

My loyal blood and loyal name;

" And all because, a yearling bride,

Homesick for English ways, I tried

To mark the sweet old Easter-tide

"Which brought upon its April way,

A year ago, a morning gay

With English bloom, — *my wedding-day !* "

A little sob at this began;

From maid to dame it swiftly ran, —

From maid to dame; then every man

Was caught within its surging tide;

The grim old elders turned aside;

The younger bent their heads to hide

Their misty eyes. A silence fell;

Then one up spoke, and broke the spell, —

"Our sister meant not ill, but well.

"Through lack of light, it seems, and not

From malice of the world begot,

Her error comes, and thus I wot

"We can o'erlook this vain display,

This popish show of Easter day."

A moment's pause — then, "Let us pray,"

He softly said with reverent air.

They bent their heads in solemn prayer,

And Christ the risen Lord was there.

WHY DOTH IT COME TO PASS?

SOMETIMES how near you are;
Sometimes how dear you are;
Then like some distant star
I see you from afar.

Sometimes through you, through you,
I see the gray sky blue,
And feel the warmth of May
In the December day.

Sometimes, sometimes I let
All burdens fall, forget

All cares and every fear
In your sweet atmosphere.

And then alas, alas!
Why doth it come to pass,
Before the hour goes by,
Before the dream doth die,

I drift and drift away
Out of your light of day,
Out of your warmth and cheer,
Your blessed atmosphere?

Why doth it come to pass?
Alas, and yet alas!
Why doth the world prevail,
Why doth the spirit fail

And hide itself away

Behind its wall of clay

Since time began — alas!

Why doth it come to pass?

TO-MORROW AT TEN.

A NEWPORT IDYL.

HOW the band plays to-night all those lovely
 Strauss airs

That I danced here last year, or sat out on the
 stairs

With Mulready, and Blakesley, and Beresford
 Brett —

" Little Brett " he was called by the rest of the set.

Tum-ti-tum — there's that perfect " Blue Dan-
 ube; " oh dear!

How I wish that Mulready or Blakesley were
 here!

What's to-day or to-night to the nights that are
 fled?

What's the rose that I hold to the rose that is
dead?

But speaking of roses reminds me of those

That I wore at the French frigate ball at the
close

Of the season. 'Twas early in breezy September,

Just a little bit coolish and chill, I remember,

But a heavenly fair night; and the band how it
played!

And how to its music we waltzed there, and
stayed

Deep into the midnight, or morning, before

We thought of departure. That rowing to
shore

In the chill and the dark I shall never forget;

At my left hand sat Blakesley, and at my right,
Brett,

Whispering soft foolish words, — Brett, not
    Blakesley, I mean,

For Blakesley was dumb.   But under the screen

Of the sea-scented darkness I saw him quite
    clear

Kiss the rose that I wore above my left ear.

Ah! as soft on my cheek I felt the light touch

Of his breath as he bent there, my heart beat
    with such

A wild pulse for a moment, that, giddy and faint,

I turned to the breeze with a sudden complaint

Of the air I found close: and the air was like
    wine, —

A strong western wind from a sky clear and fine.

It was just at that moment our boat came to land,

And I stumbled and fell as I stepped on the
    sand,

And 't was Brett's arms that caught me: I never
knew quite

What I said in that instant; I thought in the
night

It was Blakesley who held me, and Blakesley,
it seems,

Was somewhere behind, and — Oh, foolish old
dreams

Of that dead and gone time! for what do I care

For the things of last year, its mistakes or
despair,

When to-day and to-night show such untroubled
skies,

And laid at my feet is the season's great prize

For my taking or leaving; to-morrow at ten

I 'm to give him my answer, — this prize amongst
men.

Of course I have made up my mind to accept,

And to-night I must burn up that rose I have
    kept,

And the notes signed "T. B.," and must cease to
    recall ,

That foolish old time of the French frigate ball.

Tom Blakesley, indeed ! just as if I should care

For that stupid — hark ! there's a step on the
    stair,

And I told John to-night, to say " Not at home,"

To any and all of my friends that might come ;

And he's hunting me out with some card he
    has brought,

The donkey ! Now, John — Mr. Blakesley ! I
    thought —

Oh, Tom ! Tom ! let me go. How can you —
    how dare —

What ! you thought that I chose little Beresford
    there

That night in the boat, and that you —-let me go, sir,

You 're the stupidest man — A whole year!
    Don't you know, sir,

That to-morrow — what 's that? — in Egypt and
    Rome

All this year, and a meeting with Brett sent
    you home

In hot haste — and 't was love, love, you say,

And despair that sent you and kept you away?

H–m — well, it may be; but you see other men

Have not been so dull, and to-morrow at ten

I 'm to give — what is that? You 've been ill all
    this year?

Come home but to die? — oh, Tom, Tom, my dear,

Not to die, but to live; and I — my refusal I 'll
    give

To-morrow at ten; and you, you 'll stay, Tom,
    and live?

A QUESTION.

OH, was it I or was it you,
That broke the subtle chain that ran
Between us two, between us two, —
Oh, was it I or was it you?

Not very strong the chain at best,
Not quite complete from span to span,
I never thought 't would stand the test
Of settled commonplace at best.

But oh, how near, how dear you were
When things were at their first and best,

And we were friends without demur,

Shut out from all the sound and stir, —

The little petty worldly race.

Why could we not have stood the test, —

The little test of commonplace, —

And kept the glory and the grace

Of that sweet time when first we met?

Oh, was it I or was it you

That dropped the golden link, and let

The little rift and doubt and fret

Creep in and break that subtle chain? —

"Oh, was it I or was it you?"

Still ever yet and yet again

Old parted friends will ask with pain.

IN THE CROWD.

In the crowd, there she stands
With a rose in her hands;
Strong and straight, like the rose,
Lifts her head; no one knows
Of the thorn that doth prick
Her heart to the quick.

No one guesses while red
The rose lifts its head,
And its odorous breath
Fills the air, that death
With pain-poisoned dart
May be eating its heart.

No one guesses or knows

Where a proud heart bestows

Its passion and pain,

Its loss and its gain.

No one guesses or knows

What is death to the rose.

ABDICATED.

So I step down and you step up,
  Why not, why not?
I drained the draught, flung down the cup,
  And you have got
The little place I once called mine,
  And you will quaff
The wine I quaffed and call it fine —
  It makes me laugh.
You'll get so weary of the thing
  Before you 're through, —
The shows, the lies, the paltering
  Of all the crew.

I wonder if somewhere beyond

    This earthly track,

When we have slipped the fleshly bond,

    We shan't look back

With just this kind of glad relief,

    And laugh to find

That we have left the grind and grief

    So far behind?

ON THE STAIRS.

'T WAS a crowd and a crush from the time we
    began;
My tulle was in shreds, and my marabout fan
Was broken to bits as we tried to get clear
Of clumsy Dick Marlowe, who never could steer,
No matter what partner might have him in tow,
Through no matter what easy step, waltz, or
    galop.

And 'twas just in this whirl that we waltzed
    down the floor
And found our way out by the corridor door
That leads to the hall, and there on a stair,

Away from the mob and the noise and the glare,

We rested and talked and heard the band play,

With never a thought how time ran away,

Till suddenly came a great flourish and clang

Of the horns and the harps, and the clarinet
    rang

A shrill winding note like a long winding sigh,

Which we knew as we heard was good-night
    and good-by.

"Good-night and good-by?" Why, it seemed but
    a second

Since we waltzed down the room, if time might
    be reckoned

As fleetly as thoughts run, and, by the same
    token,

As fleetly and sweetly as words may be spoken.

"Good-night and good-by." Time's a thief un-
    awares.

'T is how many years since we sat on the
    stairs

And rested and talked there and heard the band
    play,

With never a thought how time ran away?

What was it we talked of, oh, what was the
    chaff,

The gay little joke that called out our laugh,

As you stooped to recover the flowers I let
    fall,

And stooping there stepped on my white Llama
    shawl?

And what was it then you murmured just after

That checked the gay joke and stopped the
    light laughter, —

What was it, what was it? I caught as you spoke
    there

One word of devotion; then suddenly broke
    there,

Just there on the stair, a sound of gay chatter

As the dancers came forth, and — perhaps —
    well, what matter

At this day and this hour if you thought I
    retreated

That moment to leave there a suitor defeated?

What matter, indeed? And yet as I listen

To the old Lanner waltzes, and see the bright
    glisten

Of yellow-gold hair on the head of my Polly,

As she sits on the stair there, I think of your
    folly

In that far-away day when you thought me
    coquetting,

While my heart was for you alone pining and
    fretting.

Well, 't is queer how one can forget and recover;

'T is twenty years now since I 've thought of the
    lover

With whom I sat out a dozen round dances,

And lost for, who knows how many fine chances —

As my daughter — Miss Marlowe — is losing out
    there

Her chances to-night on that draughty old stair.

RUNNING THE BLOCKADE.

WHEN the French fleet lay
In Massachusetts Bay
    In that day

When the British squadron made
Its impudent parade
    Of blockade;

All along and up and down
The harbor of the town,—
    The brave, proud town

That had fought with all its might

Its bold, brave fight

    For the right,

To win its way alone

And hold and rule its own,

    Such a groan

From the stanch hearts and stout

Of the Yankees there went out:

    But to rout

The British lion then

Were maddest folly, when

    One to ten

Their gallant allies lay,

Scant of powder, day by day

In the bay.

Chafing thus, impatient, sore,

One day along the shore

Slowly bore

A clipper schooner, worn

And rough and forlorn,

With its torn

Sails fluttering in the air:

The British sailors stare

At her there,

11

So cool and unafraid.

" What ! she 's running the blockade,

The jade ! "

They all at once roar out,

Then — " Damn the Yankee lout ! "

They shout.

Athwart her bows red hot

They send a challenge shot ;

But not

An inch to right or left she veers,

Straight on and on she steers,

Nor hears

Challenge or shout, until

Rings forth with British will,

A shrill

"Heave to!" Then sharp and short

Question and quick retort

Make British sport.

"What is it that you say, —

Where do I hail from pray,

What is my cargo, eh?

"My cargo? I'll allow

You can hear 'em crowin' now,

At the bow.

"And I 've long-faced gentry too,

For passengers and crew,

Just a few,

"To fatten up, you know,

For home use, and a show

Of garden sass and so.

"And from Taunton town I hail;

Good Lord, it was a gale

When I set sail!"

The British captain laught

As he leaned there abaft:

"'T is a harmless craft,

And a harmless fellow too,

With his long-faced gentry crew;

Let him through,"

He cried; and a gay " Heave ahead! "

Sounded forth, and there sped

Down the red

Sunset track, unafraid,

Straight through the blockade,

This jade

Of a harmless craft,

Packed full to her draught,

Fore and aft,

With powder and shot.

One day when, red hot

    The British got

Their full share and more

Of this cargo, they swore,

    With a roar,

At the trick she had played,

This "damned Yankee jade"

    Who had run the blockade!

DELAY.

ALWAYS to-morrow and never to day,

So the winter wears till the bloom of May:

"Yet what is a month more or less?" you say.

But as May goes over the purpling hill,

You lead before and I follow still

From end to end of the months, until

My passion wears with the autumn weather

To the very end of its tender tether;

For never apart yet never together

We walk as we walked in the bloom of May:

But at last your "to-morrow" is my "to-day,"

When, "What is a month more or less?" I say.

UNATTAINED.

TIRED, tired and spent, the day is almost run,
And oh, so little done!
Above, and far beyond, far out of sight,
Height over height,
I know the distant hills I should have trod, —
The hills of God, —
Lift up their airy peaks, crest over crest,
Where I had prest
My faltering, weary feet, had strength been given,
And found my Heaven.
Yet once, ah, once the place where now I stand
The promised land

Seemed to my young, rapt vision, from afar.

The morning star

Shone for my guidance, beckoned me along,

As, fresh and strong,

And all untried, untired I took my way

At break of day.

The path looked strewn with flowers in that
white light,

Each distant height

Smiled at me like a friend,—a faithful friend,—

Sure that the end

Would soon, ah, soon repay with sweet re-
dress

All weariness.

But when the time wore on, and in the bright

And searching light

Of high noonday I lifted up my eyes,

　　　The purple dyes

Through which I had descried my mountain

　　height

　　　Had vanished quite.

Then, suddenly, I knew that I did stand

　　　Within the promised land

Of youth's fair dreams and hopes; but with a

　　thrill

　　　I saw that still

Above and far beyond, far out of sight,

　　　Height over height,

Lifted the fairer hills I should have trod, —

　　　The hills of God!

WHO KNOWS?

WHO knows the thoughts of a child,
The angel unreconciled
To the new, strange world that lies
Outstretched to its wondering eyes?

Who knows if a piteous fear,
Too deep for a sob or a tear,
Is beneath that breathless gaze
Of sudden and swift amaze, —

Some fear from the dim unknown,
Some shadow like black mist blown

Across the heavenly ray
Of this new-come dawning day?

But the smile which as sudden and swift
Breaks through the shadowy rift, —
From what far heaven or near,
What unseen blissful sphere,

Comes the smile of a little child,
This angel unreconciled
To the new, strange world that lies
Outstretched to its wondering eyes?

WAITING.

If only the rain would cease to beat,
   If only the winds would cease to blow,
If only the clouds would beat retreat,
   And the summer sunshine glance and glow,
   I should be perfectly happy, I know.

All day, and every day, I wait
   For something or other to come and go
To make my pleasure a perfect state,
   To make my heart a summer glow
   Of sure delight that will never go.

But all day, and every day, I wait,

   And the days run by and the days run low,

And everything seems too soon or too late,

   And I never find what I seek, you know,

   Never get just what I want, you know.

There 's always something or other amiss,

   The tide is at ebb when I want it at flow,

A fleck and a flaw to mar the bliss

   That might be easily perfect, I know,

   If I could but make things come and go.

I 've waited now so long and so late,

   That the hope I had, like the tide, runs low,

And I begin to think that I shall wait

   For ever and ever like this, you know,

   For the things to come, that always go.

And I begin to think that perhaps, perhaps,

  When time is so swift and joy so slow,

I 'd better make most of the hours that elapse,

  And the best of the days that come and go,

  Or the years will be gone or ever I know.

And I shall sit weary and old and sad,

  Like a little weary old woman I know,

And think of the days I might have been glad,

  Of the pleasures I dropped, the things I let go,

  For the things I never could find, you know.

A GIRL OF GIRLS.

HERE'S a girl of girls,
Teeth as white as pearls,
Breath of balm and rose
When her lips unclose.

Look, how straight she walks;
List, how sweet she talks;
Beauty, grace, and youth
Crown her for a truth;

And along her way
Friends flock day by day,

Dropping at her feet

Showers of praises sweet.

"Beauty, grace, and youth, —

Easy 't is, forsooth,

With such gifts as these,

Friends to gain and please,"

Dark-eyed Envy cries,

Looking sadly wise

As she walks apart

With a burning heart.

Beauty, grace, and youth, —

All these gifts, in truth,

Once were Envy's own,

Yet she walks alone,

Walks in sullen pride
On the other side,
Brooding as she goes
Over petty woes,

Little hates and spites,
Fancied wrongs and slights,
Which have made her life
Dark with daily strife.

Who would care, indeed,
Follow such a lead,
Though 't were Beauty's own
Beckoned from her throne?

Sweet words match the pearls,
When my girl of girls

Doth her lips unclose,

Breathing balm and rose.

Sweet words set to deeds

Sweeter still, are seeds

Flowering day by day

All along her way,

Till to follow where

She doth lightly fare,

Is to set one's feet

In a garden sweet

Of all dear delights,

Where from heavenly heights

Friendly breezes bring

Rest and pleasuring.

THE PRINCESS'S HOLIDAY.

Up from broidery-frame and book

The Princess lifted a longing look.

Green were the fields that stretched before

The castle gate and the castle door;

And soft and clear the tinkling call

Of sheep-bells over the castle wall;

And sweetly, cheerily rose the song

Of the shepherd lad, as he strolled along

By his nibbling flocks. " Come hither, come

      hither,"

He lightly sang. " And whither, and whither

I wander, I wander, come follow, come follow!

Over the field and into the hollow! "

Down went broidery-frame and book

From the Princess' hands; and, " Look, oh,
>   look,"

She bitterly cried to her maidens there,

" At the beautiful world, so fresh and fair,

From which we are shut, day after day!

Oh, what would I give to go or stay,

Hither and thither, away at my will!

To follow and follow over the hill,

Where birds are singing, and sheep-bells ringing,

And lambkins over the grass are springing!

" The meanest peasant may have his will,

To follow and follow over the hill;

But I, because I'm a Princess born,

In tiresome state from morn to morn

Must wait, before I can go or stay,

For lackey and guard to guide my way!

Oh, what would I give to have my will

For once, just once, and over the hill,

And through the long, sweet meadowy grass

To scamper, as free as a peasant lass!"

What was it? — Did somebody whisper there?

Or was it a bird that, skimming the air,

Wickedly dropped a secret word

That nobody but the Princess heard?

For up from broidery-frame and book

She suddenly springs with a joyous look.

"And listen!" she cries, "oh, listen to me!

This is a day of victory!

For this day year the good news came

That the brave French troops had put to shame

The Spanish foe, and I heard him say —

My father, the King — that on this day,

Sinner and saint, year after year,

Should wander free, with never a fear,

On the King's highway, till the sun had set."

She laughed a light, low laugh. "'T is yet

Two hours and more ere the sun goes down,

And the King comes back from the market-town,

Where he went this morn, — two hours and more ;

And the gate is wide at the castle door !"

They pranked themselves from head to foot

In gay disguise, — a page's boot

And doublet fine to take the place

Of silken shoon and the flowing grace

Of a satin gown. Then down they bore,

These maiden troops, to the castle door.

The grim old warders frowned and stared,

The pages laughed, the maids looked scared.

But the merry girl-troopers carried the day,

For who should say a Princess " Nay "?

" But what if the King should come? " one said,

Shaking her little golden head;

" What if the King should come, alack!

Before we are safely, snugly back? "

The Princess stopped in her merry race.

" The King? " she cried, with an arch grimace,

" Let the King be told, if the King forgets,
That through this day, till the June sun sets,
The broad highway is an open way,
Where the Princess takes her holiday."

Then over the hills and into the hollow
Where sheep-bells ring, they follow and follow.
The sun is fierce and the wind is strong,
Yet " Hither, come hither ! " the shepherd's song
Beckons and beckons, now low, now loud.
But the white dust blows in a swirling cloud,
And who would have thought the way so long
To follow and follow a shepherd's song?

For it looked so near, the way he went,
When one from a palace window leant,

So near, so near, — and now so far

The palace window shines like a star;

And the meadowy grass that smelled so sweet,

How it trips and tangles the tender feet!

And the hills that seemed so smooth are set

With stubble and thorn that prick and fret.

"Heigh-ho, and heigh-ho!" the Princess cries,

As she brushes the blinding dust from her

      eyes;

"Suppose we turn on our homeward way;

It must be near to the set of day!"

Torn and draggled, the little pack

Of truant troopers wandered back, —

Torn and draggled, weary and spent,

Older and wiser than when they went.

The Princess gained her chamber door,

And out of her window leaned once more.

" Heigh-ho, and heigh-ho ! " she softly sighed,

"The world is fair and the world is wide

For peasant and prince; but let who will

Follow and follow over the hill;

I 've had enough, for one long day,

Of my own sweet will and the King's highway ! "

THE CHILDREN'S CHERRY-FEAST.

" QUICK, quick, shut the gates!" the Saxon
　　lords cried,

" And blow from the tower a blast far and wide,

To tell all the people, from courtier to clown,

That the Hussites are coming to storm the good
　　town.

" We'll teach the bold braggarts what Naumberg
　　can stand!

We'll show them how Saxon lords fight for their
　　land!

And storm as they may, from sunrise to sunset,

They'll find that we're more than a match for
　　them yet."

Outside of the gates that shut in the town,

Along by the hillsides, they came riding down, —

These handsome "bold braggarts," who laughed
    as they sped,

For bold as they rode, there rode at the head

One bolder than all, who laughed with the best,

And vowed as he laughed that this Naumberger
    nest

Should open its gates, ere the new moon was old,

To let in his troopers so gallant and bold.

But the moon of that month waxed and waned to
    its length,

And the gates were still shut 'gainst the bold
    troopers' strength.

" By my faith ! " quoth the chief, " if this be the
    way

These Saxons hold out, we must bring them to
    bay

"Without more ado at the point of the sword. "

And straight into Naumberg he sent forth his
    word,

That if, ere the end of the week had gone by,

The gates were not wide open flung, they should
    die, —

These Naumberger Saxons, who dared to deride

His soldierly fame in their insolent pride.

But the Naumbergers scornfully flung back his
    threat,

Their fortress was strong, and not yet, ah ! not
    yet

Would a Saxon lord yield to a Hussite's demand

To rove at his will through the breadth of their
    land.

Not yet, ah! not yet — but at last through the
    town

The weak wail of hunger was heard up and
    down,

And a council was called; but 't was late in the
    day

For the wise men of Naumberg to parley or pray

With the foe they had dared to flout and to
    scorn,

When their larders were stocked and their bins
    full of corn.

Ah! what should they do in this terrible strait?

They fearfully pondered behind the great gate.

Then up spoke a voice had been silent before:

"My lords, leave the children to settle this
    score —

"Nay, nay, hear me out," the rash speaker cried;

"This chief of the Hussites whom we have defied,

This iron-mailed warrior, doth keep, I am told,

A soft heart for children, like Brian the Bold.

"So what if we gather the flowers of our flock,

And tell them to speed, when the gates we unlock,

To the arms of the gay jolly chief, who awaits

To feed and protect them beyond the great
    gates?"

There was shaking of heads, and question and
    doubt,

But it ended at last in the prettiest rout

Of merry-faced creatures who thought it fine
    fun

Once more from the town-gates to scramble and
    run.

" Ho, ho! what is this? " the General cried,

As down the green path the rout he espied;

" What army of pygmies is this that I see

Coming down the green valley to charge upon
    me? "

He laughed as he spoke, and they laughed at
    him back;

Then all in a moment the whole merry pack

Flew at him and clutched him with shouts and
    with cheers,

Till his jolly red face was streaming with tears.

'T was a great joke, he thought, that the chil-
    dren should run

To the enemy's camp in their innocent fun.

Did they clamber the walls as they clambered
    his back, —

The jovial, rollicking, riotous pack?

But however they came, for the moment at least,

They were guests, to be served with a suitable
    feast ;

And what was so suitable, what was so sweet,

To serve to these runaway rogues for a treat,

As a feast of the cherries that luscious and red

Hung down from the clustering boughs over-
    head?

They crept to his knees by twos and by threes,

They swarmed at his feet like bonny bright bees,

As over the cherries they feasted together,

Down in the valley that sweet summer weather.

But long ere the end of the gay feast, forsooth,

The jolly, bold General knew the whole truth

Of the pitiful straits in the old Naumberg town;

And he said to himself, " By the King and his
    Crown,

I can't see the dear children suffer like this! "

And presently turning to each with a kiss,

He bade them good-by, 'twixt a smile and a
    frown ;

Then gathered his forces, and straight from the
    town,

When the night-shades had fallen across the
    bright day,

He rode with his handsome bold troopers away.

So the long siege was raised; and year after year

Old Naumberg has kept that summer day dear;

And year after year the children hold fête

In a gay Feast of Cherries outside the great gate.

University Press: John Wilson & Son, Cambridge.